BALLPARK
Mysteries 12

THE RANGERS
RUSTLERS

Also by David A. Kelly

Babe Ruth and the Baseball Curse

BALLPARK® Mysteries 12

THE RANGERS RUSTLERS

by David A. Kelly

illustrated by Mark Meyers

A STEPPING STONE BOOK™
Random House 🏠 New York

This book is dedicated to the parents who have volunteered their time and energy to help coach. Good coaches make good kids. —D.A.K.

For Roberta—thank you for all of your help and support. —M.M.

"One of the beautiful things about baseball is that every once in a while you come into a situation where you want to, and where you have to, reach down and prove something."
—Nolan Ryan, Texas Rangers pitcher

Text copyright © 2016 by David A. Kelly
Cover art and interior illustrations copyright © 2016 by Mark Meyers

Visit us on the Web!
SteppingStonesBooks.com
randomhousekids.com
Educators and librarians, for a variety of teaching tools, visit us at
RHTeachersLibrarians.com

Library of Congress Cataloging-in-Publication Data
Kelly, David A.
The Rangers rustlers / by David A. Kelly ; illustrated by Mark Meyers.
p. cm.—(Ballpark mysteries ; 12)
"A Stepping Stone Book."
Summary: Cousins Mike and Kate set out to catch the person who is selling counterfeit baseball shirts in the Texas Rangers' ballpark.
ISBN 978-0-385-37881-9 (trade)—ISBN 978-0-385-37882-6 (lib. bdg.)—
ISBN 978-0-385-37883-3 (ebook)
[1. Baseball—Fiction. 2. Texas Rangers (Baseball team)—Fiction. 3. Counterfeits and counterfeiting—Fiction. 4. Cousins—Fiction. 5. Arlington (Tex.)—Fiction.
6. Mystery and detective stories.] I. Meyers, Mark, illustrator. II. Title.
PZ7.K2936Ran 2016   [Fic]—dc23   2014044368

Printed in the United States of America
10 9 8 7 6 5 4

This book has been officially leveled by using the
F&P Text Level Gradient™ Leveling System.

Contents

Mike's Big Idea

"Hey, Kate, I got it! I got it!" Mike Walsh called to his cousin Kate Hopkins. He waved a blue and red T-shirt over his head and ran to catch up with her.

Mike and Kate were in Arlington, Texas, to see a Texas Rangers baseball game with Kate's mom. Mike dodged past the fans crowding the sidewalk outside the stadium until he reached Kate and her mom. "Ta-da!" he said as he held up the T-shirt.

"You finally found a Rangers shirt!" Kate

said as she examined it. "You've been looking all over for one."

Mike and Kate had spent the previous day sightseeing in nearby Dallas. At each stop, Mike had scoured souvenir stores for Texas Rangers shirts. But nobody had any. The salesclerks all said they were having problems getting them.

"Look! It's even got a hologram on the label," Mike said. He pointed to the sales tag. The label had a 3-D imprint of a baseball player. "That means it's a real Rangers shirt. I knew I'd find one!"

"Well, that's good. I'm glad you got your Texas Rangers souvenir," Kate's mom said. "Now let's go find our seats!"

Mike waved the T-shirt in a circle, like a lasso. "Woo-hoo! Let's go!" he yelled as he galloped toward the stadium. "Round 'em up, Rangers!"

The heat from the early-afternoon sun reflected off the sidewalk as Mike, Kate, and Mrs. Hopkins found their way to the stadium gates. As they pushed through the turnstiles, Mike looked confused.

"Isn't it a bobblehead game?" he asked. "Aren't we supposed to get a free bobblehead?"

"No," Mrs. Hopkins said. "We'll get a Nolan Ryan bobblehead at *tomorrow night's* game."

"But you have to be wearing something Western in order to get one," said the ticket taker. "Like a cowboy hat or a Western shirt."

"We can do that!" Mike said.

After getting through the gate, they walked to their seats. As soon as Mike and Kate sat down, Mike pointed to a four-story office building behind center field. It had windows and porches that looked down on the baseball field and big signs along its top. "Hey, if I have to work in an office when I grow up, I want to work there," he said. "I could watch every game from work!"

Mrs. Hopkins laughed. "Yes, you could, Mike," she said. "But you might not get much done." She checked her watch. "Now that you two are settled, I've got to get up to the press-room. I'll see you after the game. Have fun!"

Mrs. Hopkins was a sports reporter for the website American Sportz. She often took Mike and Kate with her when she traveled for work. The kids waved goodbye as Mrs. Hopkins walked up the aisle.

Shortly after she left, Mike popped out of his seat. "Oh no!" he cried. He searched one pocket after another.

"What's wrong?" Kate asked.

"I can't find the ten-dollar bill Grandma gave me for my birthday!" Mike said. He turned the

front pockets of his shorts inside out and shook his head.

"But what's that?" Kate asked. She pointed to a bill in Mike's right hand. "That looks like a ten to *me*!"

Mike slumped into his seat and handed Kate the bill. "It *is*," he said. "It's just not the

5

one that Grandma gave me. She had written *Happy birthday, Mike!* on the front. I was saving it, but I must have used it to buy the T-shirt by mistake! I gave the man two ten-dollar bills. One of them must have been the one from Grandma!"

Kate handed the ten-dollar bill back to Mike. "Sorry," she said. "But at least you got a cool shirt for it. And don't worry—maybe you'll get another one from Grandma next year!"

Mike sighed and nodded. He sat back and stared at the field. A few baseball players were stretching near the dugouts. Mike pulled the brim of his hat down to shield his eyes from the glare of the sun. The patches of freckles on his face stood out even more in the bright sunshine.

Kate's and Mike's seats were one section up from the field and directly behind home plate.

It was close to game time, and most of the seats were filled with Rangers fans. Many wore red or blue shirts. But here and there were some patches of green and gold worn by fans of the opposing team, the Oakland A's.

Kate nudged Mike and pointed to the third row. "Look, two empty seats," she said. "Let's try to sneak up to them!"

"Okay," Mike said. "It's weird that they're empty, but let's give it a try!"

Mike looked around. The usher at the top of the steps was busy helping a family. At the bottom of the steps, a tall man in a white cowboy hat and sunglasses was leaning against the railing. He seemed to be searching the crowd for someone. The coast was clear!

"If we can do it, maybe I'll be close enough to get one of the players to sign my baseball or my new shirt," Mike said. He held up the baseball he had brought from home. "And this will give us the perfect way to sneak up into those seats."

Mike sat in his seat and tossed the ball back and forth between his hands. On the fifth toss, he let the ball slip through his right hand. It flew over Kate's lap and bounced down the cement steps of the stadium toward the field.

Mike stood up. "Quick! Help me get my ball," he said to Kate in a loud voice as he pointed to the front of the section. Kate jumped up, and they scrambled down the steps. They followed the ball as it bounced down the steps. Mike grabbed it before it reached the lowest step. Then he and Kate ducked into the empty seats in the third row.

They pretended to rest from chasing the ball. Mike handed the ball to Kate. She held it up as if to examine it but glanced around to make sure no one had seen them sneak into the better seats.

Mike leaned over and extended his fist. Kate smiled and gave him a fist bump.

"Score!" he said.

Kate relaxed into her seat. "We did it!"

Mike tapped his forehead with his finger. "That's because I thought up a great plan."

Kate nodded. "It was a good plan," she said. "But I'm surprised, because your great plans usually involve food!"

Before Mike could respond, a strong hand clenched their shoulders and squeezed hard.

"What's the big idea there, pardners?"

Stolen Shirts!

Mike and Kate struggled to free themselves. But the hands on their shoulders only squeezed harder.

"Naaace try, y'all," said a deep voice with a thick Texas accent. "But ah think these ain't your seats."

The squeezing stopped. Mike and Kate swung around. Standing behind them was the tall man in the cowboy hat who had been standing at the bottom of the aisle.

The cowboy took off his sunglasses and

glared down at them. He wore blue jeans, a leather belt with a big star buckle, and a crisp white cowboy shirt with pearl buttons. In one side of his mouth, he clenched a wooden toothpick. He removed the toothpick and pointed it at Mike and Kate.

"Follow me," the cowboy said. He pointed to the landing at the top of the stairs. "We'll talk up there."

Mike glanced at Kate. She handed him back his baseball and headed up the stairs after the cowboy. Mike followed.

The cowboy stepped over to an open area near the top of the landing. He tilted his hat back and looked at Mike and Kate as they approached.

"What's the big idear, tryin' to sneak into those seats?" the cowboy asked through clenched teeth.

Kate's head drooped. "We just thought we'd get closer to the players. I guess we shouldn't have done that."

A big grin broke across the cowboy's face. "Maybe dur'n another game, but not today."

The man squatted down. He pulled a leather

wallet out of his pocket and flipped it open. Inside was a silver circle-shaped badge with a star in the middle. The words TEXAS RANGERS were on the bottom of the badge.

"My name's Jimmy," the cowboy said. "And I'm a Texas Ranger."

"Hi," Mike said. "I'm Mike, and this is my cousin Kate." He glanced down at the players on the field. "If you're a Ranger, shouldn't you be down there with your team?" he asked.

Jimmy laughed. "Not quite, pardner," he said. "I'm the other kind of Texas Ranger—the original."

Mike raised an eyebrow. "What do you mean?" he asked.

"He means he's a Ranger—a special type of police officer!" Kate said. "I read about them in a book I got from the library." Kate's mother took her to the library every week to get books.

Before they went on trips, Kate always read about the city they were visiting.

Jimmy nodded. "Bingo!" he said. "The Texas Rangers baseball team was actually named after *us*. Real Texas Rangers help solve crimes and keep the good people of Texas safe."

Jimmy pointed to a gray-haired man and woman in the second row of seats. They were sitting right in front of the empty seats that Mike and Kate had tried to sneak into. They were both wearing Rangers baseball hats.

"Can y'all keep a secret?" Jimmy asked.

Kate and Mike nodded.

"Well, that there man used to be the president of the United States of America!"

Kate gulped. "Really?" she asked.

Jimmy nodded again. "Yes, ma'am. He's watchin' the game with his wife, and I'm here to protect them," he said.

"Wow! That's almost cooler than being a baseball player!" Mike said. He took out his new T-shirt and a black marker from his back pocket. "Would you sign my new shirt? I was going to try to get a baseball player's autograph. But it would be even cooler to have a real Texas *Ranger* sign my *Texas Rangers* shirt!"

Jimmy smiled. "Sure," he said.

Mike handed the shirt and the black marker to Jimmy.

Jimmy placed the shirt against the nearby wall to sign it. But he noticed the price tag hanging from the shirt's neck.

"Hmph!" Jimmy grunted. He wiggled the toothpick in his mouth, reached into his pocket, and took out his phone. He typed something into the phone and then held it up to the label of the T-shirt. The phone's camera scanned the tag on the T-shirt.

Beeeeep! Beeeeep!

An alarm on the phone sounded, and a red light flashed on its screen. Jimmy checked the screen and slipped the phone into his pocket. He handed the marker back to Mike.

"Just as a'uh suspected," Jimmy said. "Ah'm sorry, Mike. I can't sign the shirt."

But before Mike could take his T-shirt back, Jimmy folded it up neatly and tucked it under his arm.

Mike's eyes grew wide. "Hey, what are you doing?" he asked. "You can't take that. It's *my* shirt!"

Jimmy shook his head. "I'm 'fraid I'm goin' to have to hold on to this for evidence," he said. "This here T-shirt is stolen property!"

A Ring of Rustlers

"What do you mean?" Mike asked. "My Rangers shirt can't be stolen! I just bought it. Let me have it back!"

Jimmy took the shirt out from under his arm and pointed to a string of numbers on the sales tag. "I just checked these numbers. This shirt was stolen from a truckful of Rangers souvenirs a few weeks ago. We've been tryin' to catch the thieves for a while."

"I thought you were guarding the former president," Mike said.

Jimmy nodded. "Yessir, we are. But we're also investigatin' a ring of rustlers," he said. "The rustlers have been stealin' delivery trucks and takin' everything in 'em."

Kate stepped forward. "Hey, wait," she said. "I thought rustlers stole cattle, not shirts."

"Well, they used to," Jimmy said. "But these days they'll take anything they can make money on, like these shirts."

Jimmy tucked the shirt back under his arm and took a notepad and pen out of his pocket. "So, where'd you buy the shirt, Mike?" he asked.

Mike studied his sneakers for a moment and then let out a long sigh. "Uhhh . . . just outside the ballpark," he said. "There was a guy with a black backpack near the corner."

Jimmy wrote something on the notepad. "Sounds like one of the rustlers we've been looking for," he said. "Can you remember anything about him? Like what he was wearin' or what he looked like?"

Mike scratched his head and thought. "Yeah. The guy had curly hair and a long, thin face," he said. "He was wearing a straw cowboy hat and a green shirt. The shirt had some type of gold logo on it. Like a star or something."

A roar went up from the crowd. Mike and Kate glanced at the field. The game had started!

Jimmy snapped the notebook shut. "Thanks, that's perfect," he said. "I'll be here for all the Rangers–Oakland A's games. Just find me if you think of anything else or if y'all see that man again. Once we catch the varmints, you'll get your shirt back."

Jimmy walked down the aisle and slipped into one of the two empty seats behind the former president.

Mike put his hands into his pockets and

scuffed his sneaker against the gray concrete floor. "It was bad enough that I gave Grandma's ten-dollar bill to the T-shirt guy," he said. "Now I don't even have the shirt!"

"Well, there's nothing we can do about it right now," Kate said. "Let's go watch the game."

Kate turned and bounded down the stairs to their original seats. Mike followed slowly.

By the top of the second inning, neither team had scored. The Rangers were on the field. The A's were batting. They had two outs and a runner in scoring position at second. One of their best hitters, Jiggs Paterson, was at the plate with two balls and two strikes.

Cliff Clinton, the Rangers pitcher, leaned forward and pulled the brim of his hat down. Behind the batter, the catcher signaled pitches with his fingers. But with a slight nod of his

head, Cliff shook off one after another. Finally, the catcher signaled a pitch that Cliff liked.

The Texas Rangers fans around Mike and Kate roared their support. They wanted that third out! Mike and Kate stood up and cheered with everyone else.

Jiggs twisted his right foot in the dirt next to home plate to get a solid footing. He glared out at Cliff and took a few slow practice swings over the plate. The cheering grew louder.

Cliff stared back at Jiggs and then, in a blur, went into his pitching motion. The ball snapped out of his fingers and hurled toward home.

It was a fastball!

As the ball approached home plate, Jiggs shifted his weight and swung.

THWHUMP!

The ball sailed right by Jiggs's bat into the catcher's mitt.

Strike three! The top half of the inning was over. The Rangers ran off the field and got ready to bat. The Oakland A's hustled out to take their positions.

Mike gave Kate a high five, and they sat back down. The Rangers were able to score a run in the bottom of the second inning and again in the third. That put them ahead 2–0. But even though the Rangers were winning, Mike was still upset about his shirt.

Kate tried to cheer him up. "Hey, I've got an idea. Let's pretend *we're* Texas Rangers and go look for the rustlers," she said.

Mike's freckled face lit up. "Yeah, okay," he said. He jumped up out of his seat. "Let's look for anyone suspicious. Like anyone with a backpack or sunglasses. And even if we don't find anything, maybe we can rustle up some hot dogs!"

Kate rolled her eyes. Mike was always thinking about food.

For the next half an hour, Mike and Kate explored the Rangers' ballpark. They saw lots of Rangers fans with cowboy hats or sunglasses and even a few with black backpacks. But none of them looked like the man with curly hair who had sold Mike his shirt. Finally, Mike and Kate went to one of the upper levels, where fans had fancy suites for watching the ballgame. Once there, Mike spotted some suspicious-looking people moving carts. The carts had black cloths covering them.

Mike and Kate hid behind a corner, watching the carts. "I'll bet those are filled with stolen T-shirts!" Mike whispered to Kate. "Maybe the rustlers have a room up here. They bring fans up to buy the stolen shirts and stuff. It makes perfect sense!"

"I don't know," Kate said. "Those carts do look a little strange. But I don't think they're filled with T-shirts."

"Well, I'm going to check it out," Mike said. "Maybe if we catch the rustlers, Ranger Jimmy will give us a reward!"

Kate stayed behind the corner while Mike tiptoed up to one of the carts. He slowly lifted the cover and peeked inside. After one look, he dropped the cover and ran back to Kate as fast as he could.

"What was it?" Kate asked.

Mike paused for a moment. He caught his breath. "You—you—you . . . ," he panted.

Kate grabbed his shoulder and shook it. "Did you see the T-shirts?"

Mike straightened up and brushed Kate's hand away. "You'll never believe what was in there," he said.

"WHAT?" asked Kate.

"Dirty dishes!" Mike said with a laugh. "A huge bin of dirty dishes! They must have come from the suites up here."

Kate scowled. But then her eyes lit up, and a thin smile crossed her face. "But, Mike," she said, "what if the *dishes* are stolen! Maybe the rustlers have moved on from T-shirts to dishes!"

Mike stared at Kate for a moment. Then they both burst out laughing.

Mike held up his hands like he was surrendering. "Okay, you got me," he said. "Maybe this was a silly idea."

"I don't think that there are any rustlers around here," Kate said. "Come on, let's get a hot dog and go to our seats."

By the time Mike and Kate sat back down, it was the sixth inning. The Rangers were still ahead 2–0. The next few innings went by quickly since neither team was able to score. By the eighth inning, it looked like the Rangers were going to win. As the teams changed places, Mike leafed through a program he had found on the ground.

The Rangers pitcher had just thrown the first pitch when Mike cried out, "Look at this!" He plopped the open program into Kate's lap. He pointed to the page on the left. There was a story about how baseball bats were made. Below that was an ad for Dusty's Steak House, a local restaurant. Mike pointed to the ad.

"I know where to look for the Rangers Rustlers!" he said. "We have to go to this restaurant! The rustlers might be there!"

Mike pointed to the Dusty's Steak House logo at the bottom of the page. It was a gold star in a red outline of the state of Texas. "I saw that logo on the front pocket of the rustler's shirt," he said. "Maybe he works there!"

Kate studied the logo. "Or maybe he just owns the T-shirt," she said with a shrug.

"Hey, it's a place to start!" Mike said. "Do you have a better idea?"

Kate shook her head. "No," she admitted. "When the game's over, I'll ask my mom to take us there for dinner."

A Surprising Change

"Y'all fixin' to be run over?" called out a female voice behind Mike. "Ya might want to find a different place to graze."

Mike, Kate, and Mrs. Hopkins had just walked into Dusty's Steak House when the tall, redheaded waitress zipped around them balancing a huge tray of sizzling steaks on her shoulder. The waitress wore a bright white cowboy hat, a shiny red shirt with fringe, blue jeans, and black cowboy boots.

Kate's mom gave Kate and Mike a nudge.

"Come on, kids," she said. "Let's see about getting a table before we cause an accident." She led them up to the hostess station. A few minutes later, they were seated at a long wooden table covered with a red and white checked plastic tablecloth. The smoky smell of barbecue drifted through the steak house.

"Hey, check out that guy at the bar," Kate whispered to Mike. She pointed to a man in a black T-shirt sitting on a tall stool at the bar across the room. "Is that the rustler?"

Mike squinted and studied the man for a moment. "Nah," he said as he shook his head. "The rustler with the backpack had curly hair and a different T-shirt."

Mike and Kate scanned the rest of the room for men with backpacks. But no one caught their eye. Instead, they watched as waiters and waitresses buzzed around the room. Lights

31

made from big wagon wheels hung from the ceiling. Horseshoes, wagon parts, bleached-white cattle skulls with long, pointed horns, and red, white, and blue Texas flags covered the restaurant's red walls. There was even a

long metal slide near the back of the restaurant that two boys were taking turns sliding down.

"Wow, this is so cool!" Kate said to her mother. "It sure feels like we're really in Texas now."

Before Kate's mom could answer, a waiter in a black cowboy hat appeared. "Howdy, y'all! Welcome to Dusty's Steak House," he said as he plunked down a big roll of paper towels. "I thought I'd bring these along since our good food is sometimes messy. Y'all look like you're from out of town. But just so you know, as long as you're at Dusty's, you're Texans to us." The waiter handed out menus. "I'll be back in a few minutes."

Mike, Kate, and Mrs. Hopkins looked over the menus. Mike picked out the "rancher" steak, while Kate picked out the "buckaroo" ribs.

"Can we go explore?" Kate asked. "It seems like there's a lot of neat stuff here."

Mrs. Hopkins smiled. "Sure," she said. "I'll tell the waiter what you want. Come back when your food arrives."

"Thanks, Mom!" Kate said. She and Mike

started with the shiny metal slide. It sat next to a flight of stairs. The sign near it read: PLEASE REMOVE SHOES WHEN USING THE SLIDE!

Mike ran up the stairs two at a time, slipped off his sneakers, and flopped down at the top of the slide. "Wheeeeee!" he called as he picked up speed and slid back down to the first floor of the restaurant.

Kate followed right behind, leaving her shoes at the top of the stairs and sliding straight down the slide. By the time she stood up, Mike was already back at the top of the slide.

"Watch this!" he called to Kate. He sat down, spun around, and slid down backward! After he popped up, he tipped a pretend cowboy hat at Kate.

"Y'all gotta try that," he drawled. "I'm fix'n to try it a'gin myself. Come on!"

Mike and Kate raced up the stairs and

down the slide a few more times, until they collapsed out of breath near their shoes at the top of the stairs. As they sat on the ground panting, Mike looked through the railing. It was a great view of the restaurant's first floor. "Hey, this is the perfect place to spy on people," he said. "We can look for the rustlers without them seeing us!"

Mike and Kate could see a row of stools at the bar area and most of the restaurant tables. They watched every time people entered or exited either area. But no one matched the description of Mike's rustler. To make sure they didn't miss their dinner, Mike and Kate took turns riding down the slide every few minutes to see if their food had arrived. When it finally did, Mike and Kate put their shoes on and bounded down the stairs to their table.

"I'm famished," Mike said as he sat down next to Kate's mom and took off his baseball cap. "This looks amazing!" One of the biggest meals that Mike or Kate had ever seen was spread out in front of them. Huge, Texas-style steaks and ribs, massive baked potatoes, and piles of greens filled their plates.

"Dig in!" Kate's mom said in between mouthfuls. "I'm afraid this looked too good for me to wait for you two."

It didn't take long for Mike and Kate to demolish their dinners. "I was pretty hungry," Kate said. She leaned into her mother's side and snuggled. "Now I'm so full I'd like to take a nap!"

Mrs. Hopkins combed her fingers through Kate's brown hair and hugged her.

But Mike pulled his napkin off his lap and dumped it on the table. "I've got a better idea," he said. "I saw some video games near the entrance. Let's see who can get the highest score!"

Kate straightened up and tossed her napkin on the table. "You're on!" she said.

Kate's mom laughed. "Well, that was a pretty quick nap."

Kate shrugged. "I guess I wasn't that tired," she said. "Thanks for dinner, Mom. Can we have some money for the video games?"

Mrs. Hopkins laughed again and pulled out her wallet. "Sure," she said. "But all I have is a twenty." She gave the money to Kate. "Don't spend it all!"

"Thanks!" Kate said. Then she handed the money to Mike. "Here, you go get some change. I'll pick out the first game that I'm going to beat you at!"

Kate and Mike got up and ran through the maze of tables. When they got to the front of the restaurant, Kate jogged to the left for the video games. Mike went to the bar on the right to get change.

Mike caught the bartender's attention and plunked the twenty-dollar bill on the counter. "Can I please have change for this?" he asked.

"I need some dollar bills for the video games."

The bartender nodded. He took the bill to the cash register. When he got back to Mike, he counted out a ten and ten ones. "That's twenty," he said. "Have fun!"

Mike took the bills and ran over to meet Kate at the video games. Kate was standing in front of a big purple and tan game that read SMASHER across the top.

Kate held her hand out. "Did you get the change?" she asked.

Mike nodded. He counted out the ten ones that the bartender had given him. "One, two, three, four, five, six, seven, eight, nine, ten," he said, placing the bills in Kate's hand. "And ten makes twenty."

As Mike gave Kate the ten, something written in blue on the face of the bill caught his eye.

HAPPY BIRTHDAY, MIKE!

A Stampede!

Kate jumped up and down. "That's the ten-dollar bill Grandma gave you!" she said. "The rustler must have used it here today!" She took the bill from Mike and tugged on his shirt. "Come on," she said. "Maybe the bartender will remember where it came from."

When they got to the bar, Mike and Kate hopped up on two stools. The bartender came over and put two napkins in front of them.

"Y'all look'n for a shot of sarsaparilla soda or root beer?" he asked.

Kate slapped Mike's bill on the counter. "No thanks," she said. "But you could help us with something else. You just gave this bill to Mike as change. We were wondering if you could remember who gave it to you."

Mike leaned forward on the rail of the bar. "He might have been wearing a green shirt with a Dusty's logo on it," he said. "He had curly hair, a cowboy hat, and a black backpack."

The bartender rocked back on his cowboy boots and thought for a moment. "Sorry, but I don't remember anyone like that being here today," he said.

Mike's shoulders slumped. He was about to slip down off the stool when the bartender picked up the ten-dollar bill and examined it.

"Ya know, most people pay with credit cards," he said. "But we do have some regulars who pay with cash." He handed the bill back to

Mike and scratched his small beard. "Now that I think about it, I probably got that bill from Buddy. He was just here a couple of hours ago."

Mike and Kate exchanged looks. "Do you know where we could find him?" Mike asked.

The bartender tipped his cowboy hat back a bit. "Shoot, sure can," he said. "Buddy's a cowboy. He works in Fort Worth at the Stockyards. It's a tourist area. Buddy runs the cattle drive in the afternoon. He's easy to spot. Just look for an older cowboy with a long white beard and a black vest."

Kate picked up the ten-dollar bill. "Thank you," she said. "That's just what we were looking for."

The bartender tipped his hat and went back to washing dishes.

"That doesn't sound like the guy who sold me the shirt," Mike said.

"I know," Kate said. "But maybe Buddy got it from the rustler!" She slipped off her stool and started for their table. "Come on," she said. "We've got a cattle drive to go to tomorrow! I'll get my mom to take us."

It was only midmorning, but the Texas sun was bright when Kate, Mike, and Mrs. Hopkins stepped out of their rental car the next day at the Stockyards. The Stockyards were in Fort Worth, Texas, about half an hour from the Rangers' ballpark. Cowboys used to buy and sell cattle there. Now it had old-time shops, a museum, a rodeo on weekends, and restaurants.

Mike nudged Kate as her mom was putting money in the parking meter. "Remember, all we have to do is find the cowboy with a long white beard," he said. "We can look for him during the cattle drive."

Kate shook her head. "I know," she said. "But maybe it's a dead end. Maybe the guy who sold you the T-shirt simply gave your ten-dollar birthday bill to Buddy as change. Maybe he was just buying a T-shirt and he's got nothing to do with the rustlers."

Mike shrugged. "Could be," he said. "But I've got a hunch!"

Suddenly, something down the street caught Mike's eyes. "Hey, look at that!" he said. Without waiting for Kate to reply, he raced to the front of the rodeo arena. Hitched to the iron fence was a huge, live brown and white Texas longhorn steer. "Come on," he called. "We can have our picture taken on it!"

By the time Kate and her mother caught up, Mike had already climbed into the extra-big saddle on top of the steer. "Yahoo!" Mike called out. "I'm a cowboy!"

"I don't think so, Mike," Kate said. "Cowboys ride horses to *herd* the cattle. They don't *ride* the cattle!"

Mike ignored her. "Watch out, or I'll have the steer stick you with its horns!"

The steer *was* taller than either Mike or Kate. And its long white horns with sharp points did look dangerous.

Mrs. Hopkins paid the cowboy who was standing nearby, keeping an eye on the steer. Then she took pictures of both Mike and Kate on top of the animal.

Mike and Kate climbed off and continued to explore with Mrs. Hopkins. Old-fashioned buildings stood on both sides of the street. They passed a museum that Mrs. Hopkins wanted to go into, but Kate dragged them farther down the street. On the other side was a cowgirl twirling a long piece of rope in a circle.

Kate, Mike, and Mrs. Hopkins watched as the cowgirl spun the circle faster and faster. *Wuuuu ... wuuuu ... wuuuu.* The rope made a whirring sound as it swirled over the cowgirl's head. With a *SNAP!* the cowgirl flicked the rope forward. The circle of rope flew fifteen feet through the air and dropped neatly over the figure of a full-size cow made out of wood.

The crowd who had gathered around to watch clapped as the cowgirl tipped her straw hat and wound the rope back up. As the crowd drifted away, Kate tugged on her mother's sleeve. "You can head to the museum if you want," she said. "But I'm going to figure out how she does that!"

Kate ran over to the cowgirl and whispered something into her ear. The cowgirl nodded. Then she taught Kate how to loop the rope into a circle using a special knot that would slip

tight once it went around something. It didn't
take long for Kate to learn how to tie the special knot. But it did take a while for her to learn
how to twirl and throw the rope.

Mike and Mrs. Hopkins waited in the shade under a nearby tree while Kate practiced. The first few times Kate tried to throw the rope it just fell flat onto the ground. But after a while, she was twirling the rope over her head, tossing it down the street, and landing it neatly over the head of the wooden cow!

After Kate had lassoed the cow five times, she handed the rope back.

"You'd make a great cowgirl," the cowgirl said to Kate. "I've never seen anyone pick up lassoing as fast as you did. Nice job!"

"Thanks!" Kate said. She had her mom take a picture of her with the cowgirl, and then they headed off to get some lunch. But before they made it to one of the many food shops, Kate convinced her mom to stop at one of the clothing stores lining the street.

"I want to use the allowance I've saved to

get a rope so I can practice lassoing at home," Kate said. "And maybe Western outfits for tonight's Old West Night. The ticket taker said if we dress up in Western clothing, we get that free Nolan Ryan bobblehead!"

"Yeah," Mike said. "I can get a hat with the money I've saved."

The three stepped inside the next clothing shop they saw. Kate quickly found a lasso, boots, and a skirt with fringe, while Mike selected a white cowboy hat, a black and red checked shirt, and a belt with a big metal buckle.

After a quick lunch, Mike, Kate, and Mrs. Hopkins lined up with the other tourists to watch the cattle drive. Mrs. Hopkins leaned against a lamppost while Mike and Kate got right up front for a good view. A few minutes after one o'clock, a cowboy on a horse rounded the corner at the far end of the street. Right behind the cowboy was a herd of huge Texas longhorn cattle. The cattle moved slowly. More cowboys rode along on each side to keep the cattle moving.

"Here they come!" Kate said. "Wow. Look at those horns. They're gigantic!"

Kate was right. The cattle looked just like the steer they had sat on earlier, but bigger. Some of them seemed to have horns that were two or three feet long.

"Pssssst!" Mike whispered to Kate. "We can look at the horns, but we really should be looking for Buddy!"

They checked out the cowboys on either side of the cattle. One was a small, redheaded man, and the other was a short cowboy with a red handkerchief around his neck.

Kate pulled her phone out and started

taking pictures as the herd of cattle ambled
by. She was just putting the phone away when
there was some activity at the back of the herd.
The people on the sidewalk stepped back.

"Watch out!" someone cried.

One of the steers had broken loose! Before the cowboys could stop it, the steer ran for the side of the street. A gasp passed through the crowd.

The long, pointy horns of the runaway steer were headed straight for Mike and Kate!

A Crazy Plan

Kate's mother screamed as the steer picked up speed.

Its hooves made a pounding sound as it ran. *Clump! Clump! Clump! Clump!*

"Quick! Get back here," Mrs. Hopkins said. Mike and Kate jumped behind the lamppost with her.

"This isn't going to end well!" Mike said.

Mike and Kate closed their eyes. The steer was so close that Mike and Kate could almost feel its hot breath. They waited to feel the collision or the sharp point of the steer's horns.

But instead, they heard the clatter of horse-shoes, the *whooshing* of a rope being thrown, and a loud *SNEEERFFFF!*

Kate and Mike opened their eyes. The steer was just a few feet away! But the cowboy with the red handkerchief had lassoed it. He was using the rope to pull the steer back to the middle of the street.

Mrs. Hopkins let out a long sigh.

"Yee-haw!" Mike yelled. He punched his fist in the air. "Ride 'em, cowboy!"

"I guess knowing how to lasso really comes in handy," Mrs. Hopkins said. She stepped away from the lamppost and gave Kate a hug. "That was a little too close for me!"

The crowd drifted back to the edge of the street to watch the end of the cattle drive. Mike and Kate sat down on the curb to catch their

breath. As they looked up, the last of the herd
of cattle passed by. The cowboy at the end was
walking his horse from one side of the road to
the other. Mike grabbed Kate's arm.

"Look at the cowboy with the long white beard!" Mike said. "That must be Buddy!" He let go of Kate and jumped up. She stood to get a better look.

The cowboy on the last horse had a long, frizzled white beard. And over his cowboy shirt he wore a black button-down vest. Thinking quickly, Kate pulled out her phone and took a picture of Buddy. She snapped another one as he tipped his hat in her direction.

"I've got it!" she said. "Now we can show the picture to Jimmy, and maybe we'll get your shirt back."

Mike shook his head.

"You mean you don't want your shirt back?" Kate asked.

Mike waited for Buddy to pass by. Then he leaned over toward Kate. "I do," he said. "But I've got a better idea. Let's follow Buddy!"

As the cattle drive continued, the crowd near Mike and Kate moved on to other things. Mrs. Hopkins checked her watch. "We have enough time to see the museum before we head to the ballpark for tonight's game," she said. "We'll stop at the hotel on the way so you two can get dressed in your Western clothes for Old West Night."

Kate looked at Mike. Mike nodded in the direction of Buddy and raised his eyebrows a couple times.

"That sounds good, Mom," Kate said. "But Mike and I really want to watch the end of the cattle drive. We'll follow the cowboys for a little bit and then wait for you outside the museum."

"Okay," she said. "Just be safe, and stay away from the cattle. I don't want either of you to get hurt! I'll meet you in about half an hour at the museum."

As Mrs. Hopkins walked down the street, Kate and Mike ran to catch up with the cattle drive. The cowboys and cattle had turned right, down a side alley with cars parked on the left. Mike and Kate stayed a short distance behind Buddy. Shortly after they turned the corner, Buddy's horse stopped. Mike and Kate ducked in between two parked cars and squatted down.

"Okay, fearless leader," Kate said. "Now what?"

Mike popped his head up and studied the situation. Then he ducked down again. "They're herding the cattle into a gate in the fence up there," he said. "They must be putting them back in their pens. Buddy will stay at the end of the herd until they're all in their gates. Then we can follow him and see where he goes."

Buddy kept moving slowly down the alley

on his horse as the cattle moved into their pens. At the same time, Mike and Kate ducked from parked car to parked car, staying hidden and following a safe distance behind Buddy.

"Psst! This is it," Mike whispered to Kate as the last of the longhorns entered the gate. When the gate closed, Buddy nudged his horse forward. He rode farther down the alley. Mike and Kate had to scurry to keep up. The line of parked cars ended at the edge of a warehouse. The warehouse had a row of doorways and garage doors. A few delivery trucks were parked on either side of the alley.

With no cars to hide behind, Mike and Kate moved from doorway to doorway, trying to keep an eye on Buddy while staying out of sight. They watched as Buddy hopped off his horse. He led it to a horse trailer attached to a red pickup truck. Buddy secured the horse in the trailer. Then he closed the back door, dusted off his hands, and walked across the alley to one of the warehouse doors. A black van was parked near the warehouse. Its back doors were open, and two men in cowboy hats and blue jeans were loading brown cardboard boxes into the van.

"What do you think is in those boxes?" Kate whispered to Mike. They were crouched out of sight in one of the doorways.

Mike popped his head around the corner for a second to get a look at the van. "Doughnuts, hopefully," he said with a smile.

Kate leaned against the doorway. She twirled her long brown hair around her finger for a moment. "Nice try, food guy," she said. "But we've got to figure out what's in those boxes for real."

Mike nodded. He sneaked another look

around the corner but pulled his head back in almost immediately. He jumped to the other side of Kate and pushed her to the edge of the doorway. "You've got to look now!" he said. "Look at the guy in the green T-shirt!"

Kate poked her head around the corner for a second and then turned back to face Mike. Her eyes were wide. "Is that who I think it is?" she asked.

"Yup! That's the guy who sold me the stolen T-shirt outside the ballpark!" Mike said. "He *is* working with Buddy!"

Before Kate could ask him any more questions, they heard a door slam. Mike and Kate quickly peeked around the corner. The back doors of the van were closed. They watched as the men went inside one of the warehouse doors.

Mike tugged on Kate's shirt. "Let's go," he

said. "We're too far away to hear what they're saying. We can hide over there." Mike pointed to a round steel garbage can near the rustler's van. It had DON'T MESS WITH TEXAS printed on its side.

"Are you crazy?" Kate asked. "It's not big enough. We'll get caught!"

A Box Score!

But it was too late. Mike was already scurrying along the side of the building. Kate ran to catch up. If the rustlers came out now, they'd see both of them.

A few seconds later, Mike and Kate ducked behind the garbage barrel. They huddled close so they wouldn't be seen. Kate was quietly panting from the run. But before she could say anything to Mike, the door to the warehouse opened. They heard voices.

"Meet me here after the baseball game with

the van," said one voice. "I've got a new place selected for the stuff. If we work fast, we can be out of here before midnight."

"Right, Buddy," said a younger voice. "See you later."

They peeked around the edge of the garbage can just in time to see Buddy get into the red pickup truck with the horse trailer. Mike's T-shirt guy and the other man in the cowboy hat climbed into the van. The van's and the pickup truck's engines kicked to life, and both drove away. A faint cloud of dust trailed behind them.

"Come on," Mike said. "Now's our chance." He nudged Kate and headed for the doorway that Buddy had just left.

The wooden door looked worn and old like all the other ones in the warehouse. Mike tried turning its handle, but it wouldn't budge.

"It's locked," Mike said. "Now what?"

Kate tried the handle, too. Then she looked at the ground. Underneath their feet was a faded doormat that read TOUGH AS TEXAS on red, white, and blue bars. She motioned for Mike to back up and then took a step back herself. "Maybe there's a key under the mat," she said.

Kate reached down and lifted up the dusty mat. The only thing underneath was concrete.

"I guess we really can't mess with Texas," Mike said as Kate put the mat back. "But it was worth a try."

Kate studied the door and the lock. Then she reached into her back pocket and pulled out her plastic library card. She slipped it between the door and the door frame.

"What are you doing?" Mike asked.

"Just something I read about in a detective book I borrowed from the library," Kate said.

She slipped the plastic card in and out along the edge of the door near the lock. "Sometimes you can unlock a door by using a plastic card to push the door latch in."

Mike looked around to make sure no one was watching. "But what if we get caught?" he asked.

Kate shrugged. "We're not going to steal

anything," she said. "We're just going to take a look." She continued working the library card along the door frame. Suddenly, they heard a *CLICK!* Kate pulled the library card out. The door swung open!

Kate's face broke into a wide smile. She slipped the card back into her pocket. "See?" she said. "I *told* you it was worth going to the library! You never know what you'll find in a book!"

Mike and Kate stepped inside and closed the door behind them. The room was dark, but a small window in the back wall let some light in. Particles of dust floated in and out of the shaft of light. Once Mike's and Kate's eyes adjusted, they looked around.

"Hay!" Mike said.

"Hey what?" Kate asked.

"Not hey," Mike said. "Hay. You know, like

H-A-Y. There's nothing but hay in here."

Mike was right. The room was filled with big bales of hay. Small green and gold strands of it stuck from the edges of the bales. The piles towered in front of the door.

Kate scanned the room. "Hay is right," she said. "But that doesn't make any sense. We saw the rustlers taking boxes from here. Let's search the place."

Mike and Kate fanned out to explore the warehouse room. Mike felt his way along the rough wooden wall on the left side. Kate examined the bales of hay stacked against the wall on the right side. Suddenly, from outside, they heard a car door slam!

Mike and Kate looked at each other. They heard footsteps on the gravel outside and two voices talking. Mike pointed to the back wall. The voices were getting louder!

Mike and Kate raced to the back of the room. They crouched down behind the last pile of hay bales and tried not to move or make any noise. But a few minutes later, the voices stopped. They heard a car door slam again and then drive away. All was quiet.

"Wow," Kate said. "That was close! We'd better hurry up and get out of here."

Mike and Kate quickly returned to searching the rest of the room. But after another five minutes, Mike gave up. He sat down on a bale of hay. The stray stalks sticking out tickled the backs of his legs.

"Hey, I'm tired," he said. "Get it? I'm saying *hey,* not *hay*!"

Kate groaned from behind a pile of hay. "Yes, Mike," she said. "I get it. They sound the same. But I could use some help here when you're done joking around. I think there's something

73

behind this bale of hay! And that's h-a-y, not h-e-y!"

Mike jumped up and raced over to Kate. With a push, they moved the bale sideways. Behind it was a pile of cardboard boxes.

"Bingo!" Kate said. "I thought there was something back there."

Mike stepped forward and pulled the cover off the box on top. He and Kate leaned over and looked in the box.

It was filled with stolen Texas Rangers T-shirts just like Mike's!

A Cowgirl to the Rescue

Kate stepped back and moved the next bale of hay away. There were more cardboard boxes behind it filled with more Texas Rangers shirts.

"This warehouse is loaded with stolen goods!" Mike said. "Buddy and the rustlers must be stealing the trucks and storing the things here. Then they load them into the van and sell them before games!"

Kate nodded. She started moving the bales of hay back into their original positions. "We've got to get to the stadium to tell Jimmy what we've found before they move all the stolen goods!" she said.

Mike and Kate finished moving the hay and ran to the door. They pushed it open slowly to see if anyone was in the alley. When they discovered it was empty, they darted out and closed the door behind them. Then they ran to the bench in front of the Stockyards museum to wait.

It wasn't long before Kate's mom met them and they headed to the car for the drive to the Rangers' ballpark. On the way, Kate's mom stopped at the hotel so Mike and Kate could put on the clothes they had bought at the Stockyards.

When they arrived at the stadium, it took a little while to get in because so many people had come for Old West Night. Fans were wearing all types of Texas clothing, from cowboy hats to skinny string ties to colorful bandannas to fancy boots. Mike and Kate fit right in. The large loop of rope coiled over Kate's shoulder made her look a lot like the cowgirl they had seen at the Stockyards that morning. Mike wore a cowboy hat, blue jeans, and the cowboy shirt and leather belt with the big buckle that he had bought earlier that day.

"Well, don't you look fancy," said the ticket taker as Kate entered. "Maybe if the Rangers start to lose, you can lasso the other team for us!"

Kate laughed. "I don't think I'm good enough to do that yet," she said as she and Mike went through the gate. "But I'll keep practicing!"

The woman handed Kate and Mike each a Nolan Ryan bobblehead. Once they were inside the park, Kate handed the bobbleheads to her

mother. "Mom, can you hold these?" she asked. "Mike and I want to look around the stadium a little. Then we'll go sit down."

Mrs. Hopkins took the bobbleheads. "Sure," she said. "I'll be up in the pressroom. I'll meet you after the game at your seats. Have fun!"

As soon as Mrs. Hopkins started walking away, Kate leaned over to Mike. "Now we can go find Jimmy!" she said. "He told us he'd be here for each Oakland A's game. Let's go!"

Mike and Kate ran through the hallways of the Rangers' ballpark until they came to the section behind home plate. They took the steps two by two down the aisle until they reached the seats where the former president had been sitting the day before. But the seats were empty today. All around them, fans were streaming in and starting to fill up the other seats.

Kate tapped her foot and scanned the

stadium. "He's not here," she said. "Where would he be?"

"Maybe the president is sitting somewhere else today," Mike said. He looked up and down the sections of seats, trying to find a tall man with a white cowboy hat standing near the former president.

"We've got to find him before the rustlers move all that stuff," Kate said. "Let's go up a level to see if we can spot him. The game is going to start in a little while!"

Mike and Kate ran up the aisle to the walkway that went around the park. They hurried along, heading down the third-base side and dodging fans while still keeping an eye out for Jimmy.

All of a sudden, Mike stopped short. "Uh-oh!" he called out.

Kate ran back to Mike. He was standing at

the railing that overlooked the field. "What's up?" she asked.

"This isn't good," Mike said. He pointed to the corner in left field. Below the main walkway was a large entranceway. It seemed to come from under the seats and open directly onto left field.

Kate followed his finger. Her jaw dropped. "What's he doing here?" she gasped.

It was Buddy, the cowboy! He was riding the same horse that Mike and Kate had watched him load into the horse trailer at the Stockyards a couple of hours ago.

"He's about to come out on the field!" Mike said. "He's probably part of Old West Night."

"We can't let him get away," said Kate. "Once he's done and comes off the field, he'll head back to Fort Worth and start moving the stolen merchandise!"

Mike made a fist and punched it into his open palm. "If only we could find Jimmy!" he said.

Kate shook her head. "There's no time," she said. "And there's no way for us to stop him. We're up here, and he's down there."

Mike studied Buddy and his horse. Buddy was holding the horse's reins. They looked like two ropes running from the horse's mouth to Buddy's hands. Mike's eyes opened wide.

"That's it!" he cried. Mike looked at Kate and her cowgirl outfit. "Come with me. I've got an idea!"

Kate followed Mike as he ran. She dodged fans finding their seats until Mike stopped at the landing at the end of one of the aisles in the left-field corner. The nearby seats were filled with fans. Mike and Kate peeked over the railing that overlooked the outfield. Buddy and his horse were right below them!

Mike took the coil of rope from Kate's shoulder and handed it to her. "Quick," he said. "Tie one of the special knots and start swinging the rope. To stop Buddy, all we have to do is lasso him!"

Kate's eyebrows tightened, and then a smile crossed her face. "That's a great idea!" she said. "I can do that!"

She uncoiled the rope and quickly tied a knot and made a lasso. A minute later, she had it whirling in circles over her head.

Wuuuu . . . wuuuu . . . wuuuu . . .

The rope circled faster and faster. Kate inched to the edge of the railing and looked down. Buddy was almost directly below her. She'd only have one chance to lasso him.

Wuuuu . . . wuuuu. . . . wuuuu . . .

The fans nearby thought that Kate was part of Old West Night and started clapping. Mike's freckled face turned red, and he backed away a bit. But Kate hardly noticed. She was too busy trying to get the throw right. She waited for Buddy's horse to stand still.

Wuuuu . . . wuuuu . . . wuuuu . . .

SNAP!

Kate flipped the rope forward.

Mike ran to the railing to watch. The spinning circle of rope flew a few feet forward and then dropped down. Kate let the rest of the rope slip through her hands. She watched as the lasso fell toward the field. But it looked like it was too far back. It was going to hit the end of the horse, not Buddy!

"Oh no!" she cried. But there was nothing she could do. The extra rope continued to slip through her hands. Kate wished she could do it over again.

But just as the rope neared its target, the horse pranced backward a couple of steps!

Instead of just hitting the back end of the horse, the lasso dropped almost perfectly over Buddy's head and down around his arms and chest. Kate let out a little gasp.

"Now!" Mike cried.

Kate quickly pulled the rope taut! The fans watched as the lasso tightened around its target. All at once, a round of applause went up for cowgirl Kate!

Down below, Buddy sputtered, "What in tarnation? What's goin' on here?"

Mike stepped up to the railing and looked down at Buddy. Then he turned around and gave Kate a high five.

"Way to go, cowgirl Kate!" he said. "You've nabbed your first rustler!"

A Surprise Signing

"Yee-haw!" Kate yelled.

"Get this rope off me!" Buddy yelled from below. "I'm not a cow!"

A few seconds later, a security guard came running up to Mike and Kate. "This isn't a rodeo, miss," he said. "That was some mighty fine roping, but you can't do it here. Somebody could get hurt!"

The security guard took the rope from Kate's hand and looked down at Buddy. A second security guard had just run up next to him.

She helped Buddy climb off his horse. Then she slipped the lasso off. The security guard near Mike and Kate coiled the rope back up.

"We weren't trying to hurt anyone," Kate said. "But the man I lassoed is a rustler! He stole a whole truck of Texas Rangers shirts."

"That sounds a little like a Texas tall tale," the security guard said. He radioed down to the guard next to Buddy. "We'll have to straighten this out back at our office."

But as soon as Mike and Kate started to follow the security guard, they heard a ruckus from below. They raced back to the railing. Buddy was swinging his cowboy hat around, swatting it at the two security guards who were trying to take him back to the office.

"Git your hands off me!" Buddy snapped. "I ain't stolen nothing!"

After a minute of wrestling, a third guard

showed up and finally escorted Buddy off the
field.

The security guards led Mike, Kate, and
Buddy back to their office. Mike and Kate had

them call Ranger Jimmy. When he showed up, Mike and Kate told him all about Buddy's warehouse of stolen goods.

"Great work, y'all!" Jimmy said. "I'll have the police check this out and take care of Buddy. Y'all should be gettin' back to your seats. I'll find you later on."

By the time Kate and Mike sat down, it was the third inning. The Rangers were ahead 3–0. It sure seemed like the Rangers wouldn't need Kate's help lassoing their rivals!

Both the A's and the Rangers scored a run in the sixth inning. In the eighth inning, the A's had a chance to tie the game. They had the bases loaded, and their best batter was up. But instead of a home run, he hit a long, high pop fly that the Rangers right fielder easily caught to end the inning.

A short while later, the Rangers won the

game, 4–1. The fans clapped and cheered as the team ran off the field. After a few minutes, people started to leave. Mike and Kate waited in their seats as the other fans left. The stadium was nearly empty when Kate's mother made it to their seats. She had a black messenger bag filled with work papers slung over her shoulder.

"I hear you're quite the cowgirl!" Mrs. Hopkins said to Kate as she gave her a hug. Mrs. Hopkins picked up the coil of rope. "Maybe when we get home you can teach me how to lasso someone to take out the trash."

Mike and Kate laughed. "I can teach you how to lasso," Kate said. "But what you lasso will be up to you."

"Well, from what I heard, I think that Kate could lasso just about anything," said a voice from behind them.

It was Ranger Jimmy. He clasped his hands on Mike's and Kate's shoulders.

Mike pointed to the seats near the first row. "We didn't see you down there today," he said. "We thought you'd be back after we saw you in the security office."

"I was in one of the suites upstairs," Ranger

Jimmy said. "Sometimes the former president sits up there with his friends."

"What happened to the cowboy that Kate lassoed?" Mrs. Hopkins asked. "And what about all the stuff that was stolen?"

Jimmy smiled. "I have to say that Mike and Kate did an amazin' job today. They cracked a case we've been workin' on for months," he said. "After the police found the stolen shirts in his warehouse, Buddy fessed up to everythin'. His gang of rustlers have been stealin' trucks and moving the goods to different places. That is, until y'all came along."

"Does that mean I can get my shirt back?" Mike asked.

Ranger Jimmy shook his head. "I'm sorry," he said. "I know you wanted it, but we have to continue to hold on to it as evidence until the case goes to court."

Mike's shoulders slumped. He nodded slowly. "Oh ... okay, I get it," he said. "I was hoping I could get it before we went home."

"I'm 'fraid we can't do that," Ranger Jimmy said. "But I talked with the owners of the team and told them how we took your shirt for evidence. And they came up with a good idea."

Ranger Jimmy reached into a bag he had set on the nearby seat. He pulled out two Texas Rangers jerseys and tossed one to Mike and one to Kate. "Since you helped the Texas Rangers—the officers of the law—catch the rustlers with a whole warehouse full of stolen goods, the Texas Rangers—the baseball club—came up with these special team jerseys for each of you!" he said.

Mike and Kate held up their jerseys. They were just like the ones the players on the team wore. The word TEXAS was stitched in thick

letters across the front of each shirt. And MIKE and KATE were written on the backs.

"Wow! These are great," Kate said. "Thank you so much!" She unbuttoned her Rangers jersey and put it on over her shirt.

"That looks great on you," Mrs. Hopkins said. "Maybe you can try out for the team!"

"Thanks for the jersey," Mike said to Jimmy. "It looks really neat. Can you sign it for me? You were going to sign my shirt before we knew that it was stolen."

Jimmy sighed and shook his head again. "I'm 'fraid I'm not going to do that, either, Mike," he said.

Mike's face darkened. "Why not?" He fished around in his back pocket and pulled out a black marker. "I've even got a marker with me."

Jimmy waved his hand at the marker and tipped his cowboy hat back. "Well, why don't you hold on to that? I know someone else who's really impressed with how you caught the rustlers," he said with a smile.

"What do you mean?" Kate asked. "Is it someone from the team?"

"No, but I think it's someone even *more* interestin'," Jimmy said. "And after I told 'em what you two did, he couldn't wait to meet you. If y'all come with me, the former president of the United States is waiting to sign your Rangers jerseys for you!"

Dugout Notes
☆ The Texas ☆ Rangers' Ballpark

Long horns. The horns on longhorn cattle can be up to six feet wide! The cattle use the horns to protect themselves against predators like coyotes.

Barbecue. Barbecue is a favorite Texas food. It is meat that is cooked over an open fire. Different types of wood can give the meat different flavors. Wood from a mesquite tree gives the meat a sweet and spicy flavor.

Greene's Hill. Greene's Hill is a wide slope of grass behind the center-field wall. It looks like a nice place to have a picnic, but it's there as a "batter's eye." A batter's eye is something that is put behind the center fielder so that the batter won't get distracted by movement or colors that might be in the background behind the pitcher. Batter's eyes allow the hitter to see the ball better when it's released by the pitcher.

Statues. The Rangers' ballpark has two big statues. One statue honors Nolan Ryan. Ryan was a famous Texas Rangers pitcher. He holds the record for most no-hitters in a career—seven. The other statue honors Tom Vandergriff, a former mayor of Arlington, Texas.

Hall of Fame. The Texas Rangers Baseball Hall of Fame, inside the stadium, has plaques of important Texas Rangers players, photographs, and other pieces of Texas Rangers history.

Texas leaguer. A Texas leaguer is a blooper (or softly

hit ball) that lands in between the infield-ers and outfielders for a single.

Mini-stadium. About one block away from the Rangers' ballpark is the Texas Rangers Youth Ballpark. It's made for kids and even has a large seating area that looks like the inside of the Texas Rangers' ballpark!

Texas tidbits. The outside of the ball-park has thirty-five steer heads and twenty-one stars carved on its walls. Texas is called the Lone Star State because its state flag has a single star on it.

Get ready for the biggest Ballpark Mystery® yet!

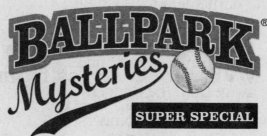

BALLPARK® Mysteries

SUPER SPECIAL

THE WORLD SERIES CURSE

The Red Sox are playing the Cubs
in the World Series! But has one of
the teams been cursed?

Find out in Fall 2016!

Got game?
Don't miss this all-new
MVP sports series from
David A. Kelly!

MVP#1:
The Gold Medal Mess

MVP#2:
The Soccer Surprise

**Get the MVP starting
lineup—available now!**

Get ready for more baseball adventure!

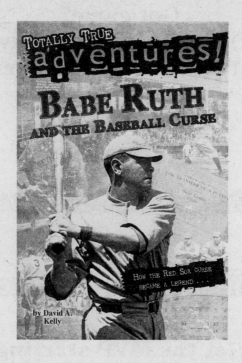

Did Babe Ruth curse the Boston Red Sox
when he moved to the New York Yankees?

Available now!